100 CATS

Cute Kitties to Count

Michael Whaite

Random House 🏠 New York

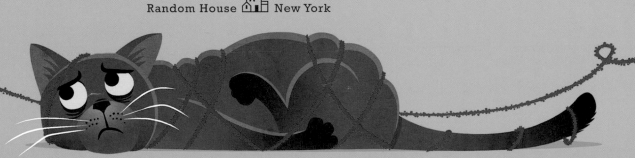

High cat, Sly cat, hide away shy cat,

leap cat,

sleep cat,

lying around the house.

Purry cat, furry cat, fast and blurry cat,

Caring cat, sharing cat, sitting still staring cat,

Welly cat, smelly cat, eating from the bin.

stretch cat, fetch cat, what have you dragged in?

Wussy cat,

fussy cat,

MEOW!

what's
new,
PUSSY cat?

Art cat, smart cat,

opening the door.

that is
not your
dish,
cat!

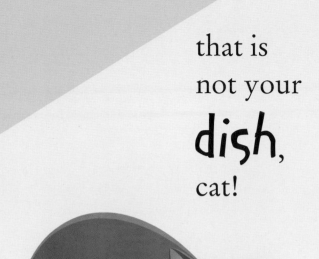

Lucky cat,

mucky cat,

messing up the floor.

Kitty cat, pretty cat, streetwise city cat,

Tabby cat, shabby cat, overfed flabby cat,

fright cat, night cat—
see his eyes glow.

jewel cat,

COOL
CAT

going with the flow.

Spin cat, grin cat, head stuck in a tin cat,

cute cat, boot cat, from a fairy tale.

Lynx cat, sphinx cat,

taking **forty winks** cat,

shed cat, shred cat,

opening your mail.

paw cat,   claw cat,

ruining your chair.

NEW cat, shoo, cat,

living in the ZOO cat,

Meme cat, Scream cat, always gets the cream cat,

styled cat, Wild cat,

never will be tame.

Clean cat,   mean cat,   visiting the
queen cat,

floppy cat,   copy cat,

looking just the same!

NOSY cat,

dozy cat,

comfy
and
cozy
cat,

sock cat,

clock cat.

TICK! TOCK! TICK!

Groom cat, ZOOOOOOOM cat,

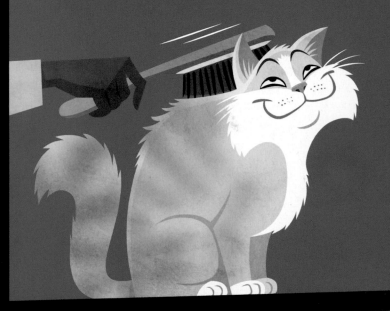 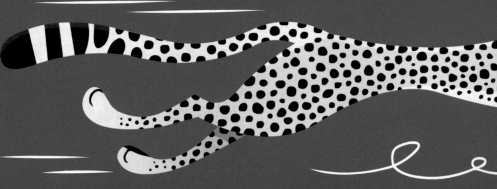

hairless cat,

flying on a **broom** cat,

careless cat—

catch
that
quick!

Flounce cat, **bounce** cat, wake you with a **Pounce** cat,

rip cat,

ship cat, sailing out to sea.

RUb cat, Scrub cat, get back in the tub cat,

Swipe cat, stripe cat, stopping by for tea.

Bad cat,

sad cat,   looking very mad cat,

top cat,

drop cat,

1st

landing on all fours.

Spray cat,   blue cat,

spy cat,

Copyright © 2019 by Michael Whaite

Random House and the colophon are registered trademarks of Penguin Random House LLC.

Visit us on the Web! rhcbooks.com

Educators and librarians, for a variety of teaching tools, visit us at RHTeachersLibrarians.com

Library of Congress Cataloging-in-Publication Data
Name: Whaite, Michael, author, illustrator.
Title: 100 cats : cute kitties to count / Michael Whaite.
Other titles: One hundred cats
Description: First edition. | New York : Random House Children's Books, 2021. |
"Originally published by Puffin Books, an imprint of Penguin Random House
Children's Books U.K., a division of Penguin Random House U.K., London, in 2019." |
Audience: Ages 2–5. |
Summary: Illustrations and rhyming text introduce one hundred cute cats of all shapes,
sizes, and personalities.
Identifiers: LCCN 2020034621 | ISBN 978-0-593-30833-2 (hardcover) |
ISBN 978-0-593-30828-8 (ebook)
Subjects: CYAC: Stories in rhyme. | Cats—Fiction. | Animals—Infancy—Fiction.
Classification: LCC PZ8.3.W532 Ok 2021 | DDC [E]—dc23

MANUFACTURED IN CHINA
10 9 8 7 6 5 4 3 2 1
First American Edition

Did
you spot
my cat?

for
Linda + David